In the Hollow of Your Hand
Slave Lullabies

When I was a child, I often heard my mother praying. As I write these songs down, I recall the words she always used to introduce herself in prayer: "Lord, it's me. I come before you, this mornin', knee-bent and body bowed, beggin' for You to hold my little chillun in the hollow of Your hand."

Hollow of Your Hand
Slave Lullabies

collected by Alice McGill

pictures by Michael Cummings

HOUGHTON MIFFLIN COMPANY

Alice McGill collected all of these songs firsthand. Every effort has been made to trace the ownership of all copyrighted material.
In the event of any question arising as to the use of any material, the editor and publisher, while expressing regret for any inadvertent error,
will be happy to make the necessary correction in future printings.

Musical transcription by Robert Friedman

Musical accompaniment (acoustic guitar, fiddle, banjo, and percussion) by Nancy Krebs

The text of this book is set in Berthold Caslon Book.
The illustrations are mixed media.

Library of Congress Cataloging-in-Publication Data

McGill, Alice.
In the hollow of your hand : slave lullabies / Alice McGill ; illustrated by Michael Cummings.
p.   cm.
Summary: A collection of lullabies orally transmitted by African American slaves
revealing their hardships and sorrows as well as soothing notes of well-being
and belief in a better time to come.

ISBN 0-395-85755-4

1. Children's poetry, American – Afro-American authors – History and criticism – Juvenile literature.
2. Lullabies, American – Afro-American authors – History and criticism – Juvenile literature.
3. Children's poetry, American – Afro-American authors. 4. Lullabies, American – Afro-American authors.
5. Slavery in literature – Juvenile literature. 6. Mother and child – Juvenile poetry. 7. Afro-Americans – Juvenile poetry.
8. Sleep – Juvenile poetry. [1. Afro-Americans – Poetry. 2. American poetry – Afro-American authors.
3. Lullabies – Afro-American. 4. Slavery – Poetry. 5. Mother and child – Poetry. 6. Sleep – Poetry.]
I. Cummings, Michael, 1945–   ill. II. Title.
PS310.N4M37   2000
811.008'09282'08996073 – dc21   97-20269 CIP AC

Printed in Singapore
TWP 10 9 8 7 6 5 4 3 2 1

To Darryl, Cannon, Jordan, Devontae, John, Matthew,
Sydney, Gina, Danielle, Isaiah, Chanae, and Symone –
my father's youngest great-grandchildren, for now.
–A.M.

To Carolyn Mazloomi for pushing me into this project.
And to all the children and parents who read this book together,
sharing the magic and love on each page.
–M.C.

THE SONGS IN THIS COLLECTION TELL THE REAL-LIFE STORIES OF A group of people who struggled to protect their children from hurt, harm, and danger. Passed down from African-American slaves in the oral tradition, these lullabies contain the essence of black survival, a philosophy designed to teach history and to counteract the tribulations of slavery with as many joyous occasions as possible.

Although the words of these lullabies often reveal the overwhelming hardship and sorrow of slavery, the musical voice strikes notes of well-being. The child, sung to sleep in loving arms, was comforted by the belief in a better time to come—if not on earth, then in heaven. Thus, "We gon' have a good time, way bye an' bye." More often than not, enslaved people were not allowed to learn to read or write, and they were punished if they were caught singing songs that did not meet the approval of the slaveholder. Many songs were shared in secret, in the woods with an iron washpot turned halfway over—the slaves believed that the pot would muffle their voices, keeping the songs in the circle and away from the slaveholder's ears. Gathering together, they strengthened one another and reported news via the slave grapevine. The act and message of the singing was "We will survive."

I was raised, with my seven sisters and brothers, in Mary's Chapel, North Carolina, a small farming community named for Mary Smith. Mary was a slave. When she was freed, she gave some of the

two hundred dollars she had saved to buy land and to build a church.

The songs collected here have been passed down through many generations. I learned them from my father and mother, my aunts, grandmothers, neighbors, and friends. They learned the songs from their parents, grandparents, and great-grandparents. The musical notes are based on my knowledge of the melodies, many of which have never been recorded.

Pa used to tell us, "Learn a song so you can keep yourself company when you're by yourself." Through music, he taught us how to think playfully and how to keep loneliness away. Sometimes he and my mother had to work twenty miles from our home. They left before sunup and we would not see them again until the sun had set. My eldest sister was left in charge. We thrived on songs like *Go to Sleepy Little Baby* and *Every Little Bit.* They reminded us of our parents' love, making us feel safe until we could be together again.

My grandmother, Elnora Stokes, said songs like *Sumtimes I Rocks My Baby* were used to make the little ones "sleep good, feel better, and have something to hope for." Grandma Elnora, who never learned to read or write, said the old folks of slavery time sang songs "not made in books" so they could remember themselves. This book is for us to remember them.

Sumtimes I Rocks My Baby

Sumtimes I rocks my baby,
Sumtimes I sees him cry,
But we gon' have a good time
Way bye an' bye.

Den I rocks my baby all the time
And keep the bad things 'way
So his little eyes will laugh at me
All the live long day.

We gon' have a good time
Way bye an' bye.

Way bye an' bye.
Way bye an' bye.
We gon' have a good time
Way bye an' bye.

Grandma Elnora often walked seven miles with a large basket of things on her head just to see us. As soon as she cleared the pine thicket, my brother Sammy would spot her and he'd sing out the good news, "Heah come Grandma." We'd leg out to meet her and to see if there was anything in her basket for us. Before long we'd hand her the baby and beg, "Sing Sumtimes I Rocks My Baby." It delighted us to see our baby chuckle along on her dancing lap and rocking shoulders.

Grandma Elnora's mother, Jane Pope Dupree, was born a slave in Tillery, North Carolina, in 1857. I was two years old when Mama Jane died.

Lil' Girl Sittin' in de Briar Bush

Come, Mammy, come.
Come, Mammy, come.
Lil' girl sittin' in de briar bush
Waitin' for de mammy to come.

Mammy done gone to de field.
Pappy done gone to de lock.
Lil' girl sittin' in de briar bush
Waitin' for de mammy to come.

Come, Mammy, come.
Oh, come, Mammy, come.
Come, Mammy, come.
Oh, come, Mammy, come.
Lil' girl sittin' in de briar bush
Waitin' for de mammy to come.

When we were children my father sang Lil' Girl Sittin' in de Briar Bush *to us if we cried for Mama. Later he told us we cried for her only if we wanted to nurse or if we wanted our diaper changed, and he couldn't do a thing about either one of those problems. We thought our father was old-timey for using the word "mammy" in this song, and we told him so. He refused to change the word – or the diaper.*

To keep their toddlers safe while they worked in the field, slave mothers sometimes built a circle of branches from briar bushes under a tree and placed the child in the center of this fortress. Other fieldworkers, on their way to get water or to empty sacks of cotton, stopped by to sing to the child.

Every Little Bit

Every little bit, added to what you got,
Hmmm . . .
Every little bit, added to what you got,
Hmmm . . .
Every little bit, added to what you got,
Will make you have a little bit more.

Every little bit, added to what you got,
Will make you have a little bit more.
Save all your kisses, sleep baby.
Save all your hugs, sleep baby.
Put 'em in a crocus sack
And shake 'em all around.

Every little bit, added to what you got,
Will make you have a little bit more.

I learned Every Little Bit *from my other grandmother, Molly Alice Pope. Ma Pope had this trunk full of all sorts of good things. Sometimes she let me hold the pretty little bottles that smelled like roses and Sweet Bessie flowers. I remember the lace handkerchiefs, old zippers, and hair combs that had carved handles. There was no end to her tray of buttons of every size, shape, and color. She saved memories too.*

I was named after Ma Pope. Her mother was born a slave in 1858 in Warrenton, North Carolina. Slave mothers often stored items that were dear and might be of use to them later. Little things like a button, pieces of string, and scraps of fabric were all protected treasures. Saving the memories of kisses and hugs was just as important.

Go to Sleepy

Go to sleep, go to sleep,
Go to sleepy little baby.

Mama gone, Papa gone,
All been sold to Georgie.
Birds and butterflies pickin' in his eye.
Poor little thing, don't you cry.
Go to sleep, go to sleep,
Go to sleepy little baby.

I'ma tell your mama, tell your papa,
Make them bad boys leave you alone.
Hush-a-bye, my baby, my baby, my baby.

My father used to sing Go to Sleepy *so softly to rock our newest baby to sleep. But when the baby cried louder, Pa sang louder. My brother Dennis would wait right good until Pa was easing him onto the bed, then suddenly he'd holler out again. Pa would have to bring him back to the rocking chair. Then Pa sang softer and softer until Dennis had really fallen asleep.*

In this lullaby the "bad boys," like the "buggah man," are larger than life. They scared young children into following the rules for safety's sake.

Dip-Dap Dudio

Dip-dap, dip-dap, dip-dap dudio.
Hmmm . . . Hmmm . . .
Heshhhh! Do you hear it?
Dip-dap, dip-dap, dip-dap dudio.
Hear it runnin',
Hear it walkin',
It's comin' . . .
For to sing dis baby to sleep.

Dip-dap, dip-dap, dip-dap dudio.
Hmmm . . . Hmmm . . .
Heshhhh! I see it . . .
Dip-dap, dip-dap, dip-dap dudio.
See it creepin',
See it crawlin',
It's comin' . . .
For to sing dis baby to sleep.

D*ip-Dap Dudio was as much fun for Pa as it was for all us children. He could make the song sound so real. When Pa said "It's comin', " I could not imagine what "it" was, but I knew something was going to appear. We never got tired of hearing him sing this song. And if we listened hard enough, creeping crawling sounds stole between the cracks in the corners of the house.*

Pa learned this song from a childless couple he was sent to live with when he was five years old. The practice of sharing children between families started out of necessity during slavery and continued for many years.

Watch and Pray

Mama's marster gwine sell us tomorrow,
Yes, yes –
Mama's marster gwine sell us tomorrow,
Yes, my child, watch and pray.

Mama's marster gwine sell us to 'Bama,
Yes, yes –
Mama's marster gwine sell us to 'Bama,
Yes, my child, watch and pray.

Yes, my child, watch and pray.

Watch and Pray *reminds me of Aunt Tempie, the granny woman who was born at the end of slavery time. Aunt Tempie delivered 215 babies in and around Mary's Chapel. All of us called her "Aunt" because she was very old, and everybody took care of her like she was kin. My mother always sent us out to play when Aunt Tempie told her stories about children who were sold away from their parents. Later on, Mama would retell these disturbing stories to us in her own words.*

This lullaby was passed down in Mary Carter Smith's family many years ago in Lowndes County, Alabama. Her great-grandparents were slaves.

Rock de Cradle, Joe

O Lulie, O Lulie,
Lemme fall 'pon your door.
Rock de cradle, rock de cradle,
Rock de cradle, Joe.

Joe whopped off 'is big toe,
Stretched it up to dry.
All de gals commence to laugh
An' Joe commence to cry.
Rock de cradle, rock de cradle,
Rock de cradle, Joe.

O Lulie, O Lulie,
Lemme fall 'pon your door.
Rock de cradle, rock de cradle,
Rock de cradle, Joe.

Joe took off 'is jimmy-johns,
Hung 'em on a rusty nail.
All de gals commence to laugh
An' Joe commence to wail.
Rock de cradle, rock de cradle,
Rock de cradle, Joe.

O Lulie, O Lulie,
Lemme fall 'pon your door.
Rock de cradle, rock de cradle,
Rock de cradle, Joe.

Joe went to de pig pen.
Slipped an' he fell in.
All de gals commence to laugh
An' Joe commence to grin.
Rock de cradle, rock de cradle,
Rock de cradle, Joe.

When my friend Dorothy moved to Mary's Chapel she was older than anyone in our fifth-grade class. She was also the most patient. That's how she became my best friend. I was the youngest in the class, but Dorothy didn't care. She whispered secrets in my ear and played games and sang songs that interested nobody but me. One of them was this nonsense song, Rock de Cradle, Joe.

Who Dat Tappin'

Who dat tappin' at de window?
Who dat knockin' at de door?
Mammy tappin' at de window.
Pappy knockin' at de door.

Mammy tappin' at de window.
Pappy knockin' at de door.

My father had a glorious singing and storytelling voice. Who Dat Tappin' *was one of his favorite songs. It was fascinating for us children who had outgrown Pa's lap to watch him sing the newest baby to sleep. It was almost like watching ourselves.*

Slaveholders on large plantations often separated children from their parents by placing them in a nursery, where older women raised them. The caretakers might comfort the children by announcing, with this song, the impending secret visit of a mother or father.

Dese Lil' Toes

Dese lil' toes gonna curl up.
Dese lil' fingers gonna curl up.
Dis lil' head gonna roll back.
Den dis baby be sleep.

Bullfrog gonna set de table.
Sis Frog gonna dip de eats.
Babe Frog gonna call his mammy.
Den dis baby be sleep.

Dis lil' nose gonna breathe in.
Dis lil' mouth gonna cry out.
Dis lil' head gonna roll back.
Den dis baby be sleep.

Bruh Possum gonna climb de fence rail.
Sis Possum gonna climb de tree.
Bruh Possum gonna drop persimmons.
Den dis baby be sleep.

Dese lil' eyes gonna shut tight.
Dese lil' ears gonna close down.
Dis lil' head gonna roll back.
Den dis baby be sleep.

Bruh Cooter gonna splash de water.
Sis Cooter gonna rake de coals.
Papa Cooter gonna find de needle.
Den dis baby be sleep.

A long time ago in Mary's Chapel a mother and her newborn were confined to the house for nine days after the birth. After that, a wise elderly woman "carried the baby out." This woman cradled the bundled baby on her shoulder and stepped outside. For fifteen or twenty minutes, she talked in a quiet voice. She told the baby to get book learning and not to dwell in foolishness. She predicted that the baby would lead a good and fruitful life. Then she returned to the house and sang the baby to sleep.

Dese Lil' Toes *was one of the songs that ended the confinement period for my youngest brother, Dennis.*

Liddy Lay Low

Liddy, lay low.
Liddy, lay low, my purty lil' baby,
Don't you cry, don't you cry.
Jest you wait for the angel's band
Way up yonder in the hollow of His hand.

Ol' Marster gwine suck sorrow.
Liddy, lay low.
Ol' Marster gwine suck sorrow.
Liddy, lay low.

De time is now.
De time is now.
Oh and it won't be long.
Wipe your eyes. Wipe your eyes.
Dey gon' take us to dat man.
Way over yonder in the Promised Land.

Ol' Marster gwine suck sorrow.
Liddy, lay low.
Ol' Marster gwine suck sorrow.
Liddy, lay low.

Liddy, lay low.
Liddy, lay low, my purty lil' baby,
Don't you cry, don't you cry.
Jest you wait for the angel's band
Way up yonder in the hollow of His hand.

When Mister Jesse Bee returned from serving in World War I he laughed to my father, "Bruh Sam, do you know a baby song brought me back home?" He recalled how his mother, who was born a slave, sang Liddy Lay Low *to him as a child, and how the song popped into his head one night as gun shells exploded all around his foxhole. A lot of men died that night. From then on this little song gave him courage.*

Great Big Dog

Great big dog come a runnin' down de river,
Shook his tail an' jarred de meadow.
Go 'way, ol' dog, go 'way, ol' dog.
You shan't have my baby.

Mama loves you, Papa loves you,
Ev'ybody loves baby.
Mama loves you, Papa loves you,
Ev'ybody loves baby.

Great big dog come sniffin' through de woods,
Batted his eye, and knocked down de trees.
Go 'way, ol' dog, go 'way, ol' dog.
You shan't have my baby.

Mama loves you, Papa loves you,
Ev'ybody loves baby.
Mama loves you, Papa loves you,
Ev'ybody loves baby.

Great big dog come stompin' down de road,
Stepped so hard he knocked down de houses.
Go 'way, ol' dog, go 'way, ol' dog.
You shan't have my baby.

Mama loves you, Papa loves you,
Ev'ybody loves baby.
Mama loves you, Papa loves you,
Ev'ybody loves baby.

My Aunt Susie sang Great Big Dog *to comfort me when I was four years old. My parents had sent me to her house because my mother was getting ready to have a new baby. Now in the old days, children were told that babies came from stump holes. My mother was heavyset, so I didn't know she was carrying a baby. But I did know that babies didn't come from stump holes. I checked out every one I saw. Never did see a baby in any one of them.*

Aunt Susie collected songs and poems. She learned this lullaby from her father-in-law, Bob Shields. Bruh Bob's grandparents were slaves in Scotland Neck, North Carolina.

Big-Eyed Baby

Go to sleepy, little baby, baby.
So de buggah won't catch you, catch you.
Mama and Papa gone away.
Leave nobody but de big-eyed baby, baby.

Go to sleepy, little baby, baby.
So de buggah won't catch you, catch you.
Mama and Papa gone away.
Leave nobody but de big-eyed baby.

Big-Eyed Baby *was passed along in my sister-in-law Mattie McGill Barnes's family. As a child she sang this song to her younger sisters and brothers in South Carolina. There were twelve of them in all, counting my husband. The beautiful little tune of this lullaby made them forget their fears of the buggah man.*

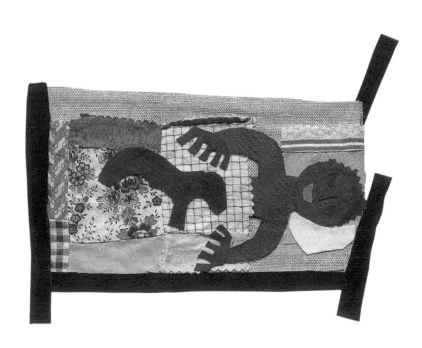

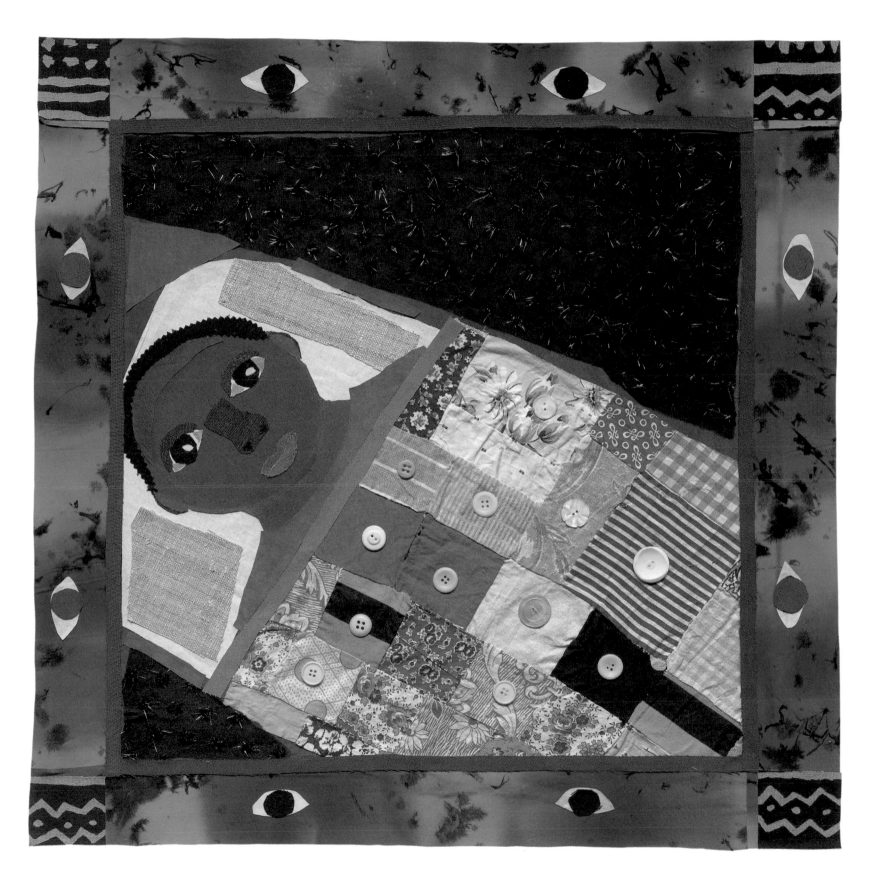

Hush-a Little Baby

Hush-a little baby, don't you cry.
You know your mama was born to die.
But you gon' see her bye an' bye
Way up yonder in the middle of the sky.
He gon' shake her righteous hand.
Good Lawd, Lawd, Lawd.

Poor little lambie, dry your eye.
I done told you she was born to die.
But you gon' see her bye an' bye
Way up yonder in the middle of the sky.
He gon' shake her righteous hand.
Good Lawd, Lawd, Lawd.

Motherless children, look up high.
You know your mama may hear your cry.
But you gon' see her bye an' bye
Way up yonder in the middle of the sky.
He gon' shake her righteous hand.
Good Lawd, Lawd, Lawd.

I just come here to sing this song.
Children, don't you know me,
Don't you do me no harm.
You gon' see her bye an' bye
Way up yonder in the middle of the sky.

He gon' shake her righteous hand.
Good Lawd, Lawd, Lawd.

*E*verybody in the neighborhood addressed Mister Joseph Clarence Smith as "Bruh Joe." He and his wife, Miss Fannie, were considered the local historians in Mary's Chapel. Bruh Joe was in his eighties when I scratched Hush-a Little Baby *from his memory. At that time I thought I knew everything, so I asked him why anybody would sing a song about death to children. I'll never forget his reply. "If you can't own up to death when you're young, you'll never live to get old." Bruh Joe lived to be 106.*

About the Lullabies

The basic melodies of the lullabies are provided here as I learned and remember them. As is true of most African-American folk songs, particularly field hollers and spirituals, singers often added words and phrases that best suited life situations or the mood of the moment. Changes also occurred in the music as the songs traveled from plantation to plantation throughout the South, forever keeping to the African drumbeat. Knowledgeable musicians have defined terms such as syncopation, the pentatonic scale, polyrhythm, 4/4 meter, and the "blue note." To be sure, some of these terms can be applied to the slave lullabies, yet the musical notation leaves room for improvisation and the individual emotional expression of the singer's voice.

The old folks of Mary's Chapel used to say, "You ain't got to 'sing like angels or preach like Paul.'"* This writer must follow the ways of the old folks who went on to define good singing as "snatching it back and making it plain."

*From "Balm in Gilead," a Negro spiritual.

Sumtimes I Rocks My Baby

Sum - times I rocks my ba - by, Sum - times I sees hi - m cry, But we gon' have a good ti - me Wa - y bye an' bye. Den I rocks my b- a - by all the ti - me And keep the ba - d things 'way So his lit - tle eyes will laugh at m - e All the li - ve lo - ng day. We gon' have a good ti - me Wa - y bye an' bye. Way by - e an' bye. Wa - y bye an' bye. We gon' have a good ti - me Wa - y bye an' bye.

Lil' Girl Sittin' in de Briar Bush

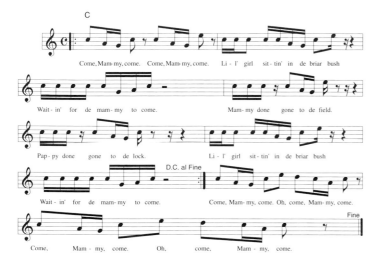

Come, Mam-my, come. Come, Mam-my, come. Li - l' girl sit - tin' in de briar bush

Wait - in' for de mam-my to come. Mam-my done gone to de field.

Pap - py done gone to de lock. Li - l' girl sit - tin' in de briar bush

Wait - in' for de mam-my to come. Come, Mam-my, come. Oh, come, Mam-my, come.

Come, Mam-my, come. Oh, come, Mam-my, come.

Every Little Bit

Eve - ry lit - tle bit, ad - ded to what you got,

Hmmm. . . Eve - ry

lit - tle bit, ad - ded to what you got, Will make you have a

lit - tle bit more. Eve - ry lit - tle bit,

ad - ded to what you got, Will make you have a lit - tle bit more.

Save all your kis - ses, sleep ba - by. Save all your hugs, sleep

ba - by. Put 'em in a cro - cus sack And shake 'em all a - round.

Eve - ry lit - tle bit, ad - ded to what you got, Will make you have a lit - tle bit more.

Go to Sleepy

Go to sle-ep, go to sle-ep, Go to slee-py lit-tle b-a-by.

Ma-ma gone, Pa-pa gone, All been sold to Ge-o-r-gie.

Birds and but-ter-flies pic-kin' in his eye. Poor lit-tle thi-ng, do-n't yo-u cry.

Go to sle-ep, go to sle-ep, Go to slee-py lit-tle b-a-by.

I'm-a tell you-r ma-ma, tell you-r pa-pa,

Make the-m bad boys leave you a-lo-ne. Hush-a-bye, my

ba-by, my ba-by, my ba-by.

Dip-Dap Dudio

Dip-dap, dip-dap, dip-dap du-di-o.

Hm-mm . . . Hm-mm . . .

Heshhhh! Do you hear it?

Dip-dap, dip-dap, dip-dap

du-di-o. Hear it run-nin', Hear it

wal-kin', It's com-in' . . . For to

sing dis ba-by to sleep.

Repeat for verse 2

2) Dip-dap, dip-dap, dip-dap dudio.
Hmmm . . . Hmmm . . .
Heshhhh! I see it . . .
Dip-dap, dip-dap, dip-dap dudio.
See it creepin',
See it crawlin',
It's comin' . . .
For to sing dis baby to sleep.

Watch and Pray

Ma-ma's mar-ster gwine sell us to-mor-row, Yes, yes --

Ma-ma's mar-ster gwine sell us to-mor-row, Yes,

my child, watch and pray. Mama's mar-ster gwine sell us to-

mor-row, Yes, yes -- Ma-ma's mar-ster gwine sell us to-

mor-row, Yes, my child, watch and pray.

Ma-ma's mar-ster gwine sell us to-mor-row, Yes,

yes -- Ma-ma's mar-ster gwine sell us to-

mor-row, Yes, my child, watch and pray.

Fine | D.S. al Fine

Ma - ma's

2) Mama's marster gwine sell us to 'Bama,
   Yes, yes--
   Mama's marster gwine sell us to 'Bama,
   Yes, my child, watch and pray.

Rock de Cradle, Joe

O Lu - lie, O Lu - lie,

Lem - me fall 'pon your door.

Rock de cra-dle, rock de cra-dle, Rock de cra-dle, Joe.

Joe whopped off 'is big toe,

Stretched it u-p to dry. All de gals com-mence

to laugh An' Joe com-mence t-o cry.

Repeat for verses 2 and 3

Rock de cra-dle, rock de cra-dle, Rock de cra-dle, Joe.

2) O Lulie, O Lulie,
   Lemme fall 'pon your door.
   Rock de cradle, rock de cradle,
   Rock de cradle, Joe.
   Joe took off 'is jimmy-johns,
   Hung 'em on a rusty nail.
   All de gals commence to laugh
   An' Joe commence to wail.
   Rock de cradle, rock de cradle,
   Rock de cradle, Joe.

3) O Lulie, O Lulie,
   Lemme fall 'pon your door.
   Rock de cradle, rock de cradle,
   Rock de cradle, Joe.
   Joe went to de pig pen.
   Slipped an' he fell in.
   All de gals commence to laugh
   An' Joe commence to grin.
   Rock de cradle, rock de cradle,
   Rock de cradle, Joe.

Who Dat Tappin'

Who dat tap-pin' at de win-dow?

Who dat knock-in' at de door?   Mam-my tap-pin' at de win-dow.

Repeat 3 more times

Pap-py knock-in' at de door.

Dese Lil' Toes

Dese lil' toes gon-na cur-l up.

Dese lil' fin-gers gon-na cur-l up.

Dis lil' head gon-na roll back.

Den dis ba-by be sleep.   Bull-frog gon-na

set de ta-ble.   Sis Frog gon-na dip de eats.

Babe Frog gon-na call his mam-my.

Repeat for verses 2-5

Den dis ba-by be sleep.

2) Dis lil' nose gonna breathe in.
   Dis lil' mouth gonna cry out.
   Dis lil' head gonna roll back.
   Den dis baby be sleep.

3) Bruh Possum gonna climb de fence rail.
   Sis Possum gonna climb de tree.
   Bruh Possum gonna drop persimmons.
   Den dis baby be sleep.

4) Dese lil' eyes gonna shut tight.
   Dese lil' ears gonna close down.
   Dis lil' head gonna roll back.
   Den dis baby be sleep.

5) Bruh Cooter gonna splash de water.
   Sis Cooter gonna rake de coals.
   Papa Cooter gonna find de needle.
   Den dis baby be sleep.

Liddy Lay Low

Great Big Dog

2) Great big dog come sniffin' through de woods,
Batted his eye, and knocked down de trees.
Go 'way, ol' dog, go 'way, ol' dog.
You shan't have my baby.

3) Great big dog come stompin' down de road,
Stepped so hard he knocked down de houses.
Go 'way, ol' dog, go 'way, ol' dog.
You shan't have my baby.

Big-Eyed Baby

Go to slee-py, lit-tle ba by,
ba by. So de bug-gah wo-n't catch you,
catch you. Ma-ma and Pa-pa gone a-way.
Leave no-bo-dy but de big-eyed
ba by, ba by.

Repeat once

Hush-a Little Baby

Hush-a lit-tle b-a-by, don't you cry. You
know your ma-ma was born to die. But
you gon' see her bye an' bye Way up yon-der in the
mid-dle of the sky. He gon' shake her right-eous ha-nd.
Good Lawd, La-wd, Lawd.

Repeat for verses 2-4

2) Poor little lambie, dry your eye.
I done told you she was born to die.
But you gon' see her bye an' bye
Way up yonder in the middle of the sky.
He' gon shake her righteous hand.
Good Lawd, Lawd, Lawd.

3) Motherless children, look up high.
You know your mama may hear your cry.
But you gon' see her bye an' bye
Way up yonder in the middle of the sky.
He' gon shake her righteous hand.
Good Lawd, Lawd, Lawd.

4) I just come here to sing this song.
Children, don't you know me, Don't you do me no harm.
You gon' see her bye an' bye
Way up yonder in the middle of the sky.
He' gon shake her righteous hand.
Good Lawd, Lawd, Lawd.